A World of Recipes

The Caribbean

Julie McCulloch

Heinemann
Library
Chicago, Illinois

© 2001 Reed Educational & Professional Publishing
Published by Heinemann Library,
an imprint of Reed Educational & Professional Publishing,
Chicago, IL

Customer Service 888-454-2279
Visit our website at www.heinemannlibrary.com

Designed by Tinstar Design
Illustrations by Nicholas Beresford-Davies
Originated by Dot Gradations
Printed by Wing King Tong in Hong Kong.

05 04 03 02 01
10 9 8 7 6 5 4 3 2

Acknowledgments
The Publishers would like to thank the following for permission to reproduce photographs:
Anthony Blake Photo Library, p.6; Robert Harding, p.5; All other photographs: Gareth Boden.
Illustration p.45, US Department of Agriculture/US Department of Health and Human Services.

Cover photographs reproduced with permission of Gareth Boden.

Some words in this book are in bold, **like this.** You can find out what they mean by looking in the glossary.

Contents

Key

* easy

** medium

*** difficult

Caribbean Food

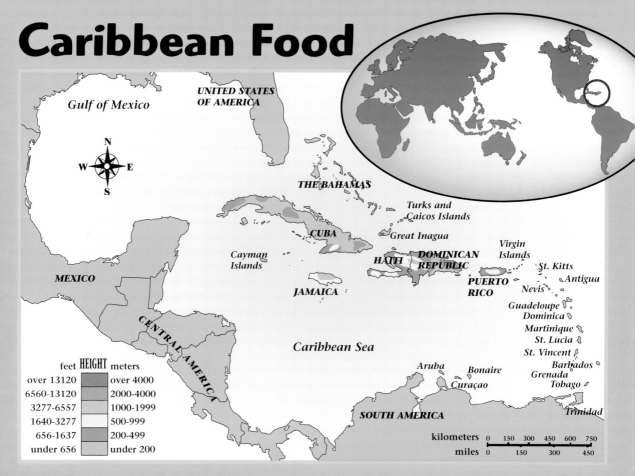

The Caribbean is a large area off the east coast of Central America. It is made up of many different countries. There are hundreds of islands in the Caribbean. Some of them are very large; others are so small that no one lives on them.

In the past

The Caribbean islands were originally inhabited by groups of Native American Indians, first by the Arawaks and then the Caribs. These people grew corn, sweet potatoes, and peppers and caught fish.

In the fifteenth century, European explorers began to travel to the Caribbean. People from Spain, Britain, France, and Holland settled on the islands. They began to grow sugar on huge farms called plantations. The settlers realized that they needed people to work on these plantations, so they captured men, women, and children from Africa and brought them across to the

Caribbean as slaves. The African people brought with them their own traditions and ways of cooking. At the end of the nineteenth century, slavery became illegal. The slaves left the sugar plantations and started their own farms. They grew different crops, such as cocoa and bananas.

This is a typical sugar plantation in the Caribbean.

Climate around the Caribbean

The climate varies among the different islands in the Caribbean. It is generally warm, but some islands are lush and green, while others are almost like deserts. Each area grows different crops. Coconuts, bananas, mangoes, oranges, limes, lemons, pineapples, and papayas grow on many islands. On the desertlike islands, people use local vegetables such as sweet potatoes, pumpkin, and even cactus to create colorful and tasty meals.

Caribbean meals

A traditional Caribbean meal has three courses—an appetizer, a main course, and a dessert. The appetizer might be vegetables or fruit made into a soup or **deep-fried** and served with a salad. The main course is often a meat dish—usually chicken, pork, or goat, often served with rice. Desserts are usually very sweet and often include coconut or fruit.

5

Ingredients

sweet potato

pumpkin

mango

coconut

lime

banana

coconut milk

ginger

cinnamon

nutmeg

Many ingredients for Caribbean recipes are easy to find in grocery stores and supermarkets.

Coconut

Coconuts grow all over the Caribbean and are used in hundreds of different ways in Caribbean cooking. You can sometimes find fresh coconuts in grocery stores and supermarkets. Packages of flaked coconut and cans of coconut milk are easy to find as well. Coconut milk is made by **grating** the flesh of the coconut and mixing it with water. The **transparent** juice inside the coconut is a popular Caribbean drink, too.

6

Fruit

The climate of the Caribbean is ideal for growing all kinds of fruit. This book includes recipes that use some of the most common Caribbean fruits—bananas, mangoes, and limes.

Plantains

Plantains are members of the banana family. They are bigger and firmer than bananas and need to be cooked before they can be eaten. If you have trouble finding plantains, you can use unripe, green bananas instead.

plantain

Pumpkins

Pumpkins are grown all over the Caribbean. They are a **staple** ingredient in many dishes, both sweet and **savory**. If you can't find pumpkin, you can use any kind of squash, such as butternut squash, instead.

Spices

Spices are plants or seeds with strong flavors that are used to add taste in cooking. Caribbean cooks use many spices. Some of the most common are cinnamon, nutmeg, ginger, allspice, and chili powder. Chili powder is very hot and spicy, so leave it out if you don't like spicy food. All of these spices are easy to find and can be bought dried.

Sweet potatoes

Sweet potatoes have an orange or red skin and orange flesh. They come from a different plant than white potatoes and are used in many Caribbean dishes.

Before You Begin

Kitchen rules

There are a few basic rules you should always follow when you cook:

- Ask an adult if you can use the kitchen.
- Some cooking processes, especially those involving hot water or oil, can be dangerous. When you see this sign, take extra care or ask an adult to help.
- Wash your hands before you begin.
- Wear an apron to protect your clothes. Tie back long hair.
- Be very careful when using sharp knives.
- Never leave pan handles sticking out—it could be dangerous if you bump into them.
- Always wear oven mitts when lifting things in and out of the oven.
- Wash fruits and vegetables before using them.

How long will it take?

Some of the recipes in this book are quick and easy, and some are more difficult and take longer. The strip across the top of the right-hand page of each recipe tells you how long it takes to cook the dish from start to finish. It also shows how difficult each dish is to make: * (easy), ** (medium), or *** (difficult).

Quantities and measurements

You can see how many people each recipe will serve at the top of the right-hand page, too. Most of the recipes in this book make enough to feed two people. A few of the recipes make enough for four. You can multiply or divide the quantities if you want to cook for more or fewer people.

8

Ingredients for recipes can be measured in two different ways. Imperial measurements use cups, ounces, and fluid ounces. Metric measurements use grams and milliliters.

In the recipes you will see the following abbreviations:

tbsp = tablespoon   oz = ounce
tsp = teaspoon   lb = pound
ml = milliliters   cm = centimeters
g = gram

Utensils

To cook the recipes in this book, you will need these utensils as well as kitchen essentials, such as spoons, plates, and bowls:

- 1 8-in. (20-cm) round baking pan
- 1 loaf pan
- cutting board
- cooling rack
- foil
- food processor or blender
- frying pan
- grater
- large bowl
- large, flat ovenproof dish
- lemon squeezer
- measuring cup
- metal or wooden skewers
- roasting pan
- rolling pin
- saucepan with lid
- measuring spoons
- sharp knife
- sieve or colander
- small bowl
- wooden spoon

Whenever you use kitchen knives, be very careful.

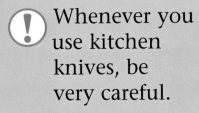

9

Pumpkin Soup

What you need

1 garlic clove
$1/2$ onion
$2 1/4$ lb. (1 kg) fresh
   pumpkin, or 3 cups
   (500 g) canned
   pumpkin
1 carrot
1 vegetable **bouillon
   cube**
1 tbsp vegetable oil
$1/2$ tsp chili powder
   (optional)
$1/4$ tsp dried ginger
$1/4$ tsp cinnamon
$1/4$ tsp allspice
1 14-oz (400-ml) can
   coconut milk
salt and pepper

Pumpkin is used in both **savory** and sweet dishes in the Caribbean. Although pumpkin is actually a fruit, it is usually cooked like a vegetable.

What you do

1 **Peel** the garlic clove and onion and finely **chop** them.

2 If using fresh pumpkin, carefully cut it into quarters. Lay each quarter flat on a cutting board and carefully peel it as shown below. Use a spoon to scoop out the seeds, then chop the pumpkin into bite-sized chunks.

3 Wash the carrot and chop it into pieces about the same size as the pumpkin chunks.

4 Pour 2 cups (500 ml) of water into a saucepan and bring it to a **boil**. Drop the bouillon cube into the water and stir it until it **dissolves**. Remove the **stock** from the heat.

10

⚠ **5** Heat the oil in a saucepan over medium heat. Add the chopped onion and garlic and chili powder (if using) and **fry** for 3 minutes.

6 Stir in the ginger, cinnamon, allspice, coconut milk, stock, and a pinch of salt and pepper.

7 Bring the soup to a boil, then **simmer** it for 5 minutes. Add the carrot pieces and pumpkin chunks and bring the soup to a boil again.

8 **Cover** the pan and cook the soup over low heat for 40 minutes.

⚠ **9** Carefully pour the hot soup into a food processor or blender and **blend** it on the highest setting until it is smooth.

Banana Soup

In the Caribbean, this soup is usually made with another member of the banana family, plantains. Plantains need to be cooked before they can be eaten. Bananas that are not yet completely ripe and are still slightly green make a good substitute in this dish.

What you need

2 unripe bananas
1 vegetable **bouillon cube**
1 cup (200 ml) canned coconut milk
salt and pepper
1/4 tsp chili powder (optional)

What you do

1 Put 2 cups (500 ml) of water into a saucepan and bring it to a **boil.** Drop the bouillon cube into the water and stir until it **dissolves.** Remove the **stock** from the heat.

2 **Peel** the bananas and **slice** them.

12

3 Put the sliced bananas, stock, coconut milk, chili powder (if using), and a pinch of salt and pepper into a saucepan.

4 Bring the soup to a boil. **Cover** the pan and cook the soup over low heat for 10 minutes.

(!) 5 Pour the hot soup into a food processor or blender and blend it on the highest setting until it is smooth.

SATURDAY SOUPS

Soup is popular on nearly all the Caribbean islands. It is often served on Saturday mornings to use up leftovers before cooking a big Sunday lunch the next day.

Chicken and Banana Skewers

For this dish, pieces of chicken and banana are threaded onto sticks called "skewers" and **broiled**. As with banana soup on page 12, this dish often is made with plantains in the Caribbean. This recipe uses unripe bananas that are still slightly green.

What you need

1 tbsp smooth peanut butter
1 tsp paprika
$1/4$ tsp dried ginger
1 boneless, skinless chicken breast
2 unripe bananas

What you do

1 Put the peanut butter, paprika, and ginger in a saucepan and add 3 tbsp of water. Heat gently over low heat until the peanut butter has melted into the other ingredients. Pour the sauce into a bowl.

2 Cut the chicken into small pieces. Put the chicken pieces into the bowl with the sauce and mix well so the chicken is coated with the sauce. Leave it to **marinate** in the sauce for 1 hour.

3 **Peel** the bananas and thickly **slice** them.

14

4 Take the chicken pieces out of the sauce. Push a piece of chicken and a piece of banana onto a skewer. Repeat until the skewer is full. Make three more.

5 Brush the chicken and banana with leftover sauce.

6 Grill the skewered chicken and banana over medium heat for 10 minutes, turning halfway through, until they are golden brown and the chicken is cooked through.

VEGETARIAN VARIATION

Try making vegetarian skewers by replacing the chicken with pieces of pumpkin or sweet potato. Cut the vegetables into pieces and **boil** them in water for 10 minutes before marinating them in the same way as the chicken.

15

Chicken in Coconut Sauce

Coconuts grow on most Caribbean islands and are used in many dishes. Both their flesh and their milk are very **nutritious**. In this dish, coconut milk makes a creamy sauce for the chicken.

What you need

2 boneless, skinless
   chicken breasts
1 garlic clove
$1/2$ onion
2 green onions
1 tbsp vegetable oil
$1/4$ tsp chili powder
   (optional)
$1/4$ tsp curry powder
$1/2$ tsp dried thyme
1 $1/3$ cup (300 ml)
   canned coconut
   milk

What you do

1 **Chop** the chicken breasts into small pieces.

2 **Peel** the garlic clove and onion and finely chop them.

3 Cut the tops and bottoms off the green onions and finely chop the rest.

4 Heat the oil in a saucepan. Add the chicken pieces, chopped garlic and onion, chili powder (if using), and curry powder.

5 **Fry** the mixture for 10 minutes, stirring from time to time.

6 Add the chopped green onions, thyme, and coconut milk to the saucepan.

7 Bring the mixture to a **boil**, then reduce the heat and **simmer** for about 40 minutes, until the sauce has thickened.

8 Serve with plain rice.

Fish and Shrimp Bake

The sea around the Caribbean islands provides a lot of fish. This recipe makes enough to feed four people. You can use fresh or frozen fish. If you use frozen fish, make sure you move it from the freezer to the refrigerator about 12 hours before you start cooking so it can completely **thaw**.

What you need

2 garlic cloves
2 onions
1 eggplant
4 medium potatoes
1/3 lb (150 g) cabbage
1/2 lb (240 g) pumpkin
4 fish fillets
1/2 cup (100 ml) olive oil
1/2 tsp chili powder (optional)
1 small bunch fresh parsley
1/2 lb (240 g) peeled shrimp

What you do

1 **Preheat** the oven to 375°F (190°C).

2 **Peel** the garlic and onions and finely **chop** them.

3 Chop the eggplant about 1/2 in. (1 cm) thick.

4 Peel or scrub the potatoes and thinly **slice** them.

5 Finely shred the cabbage.

6 Peel the pumpkin, remove the seeds, and cut it into pieces about 1/2 in. (1 cm) across.

7 Finely chop the parsley.

8 Put the fish into a saucepan. Cover it with water, bring to a **boil**, and then **simmer** for about 5 minutes.

⚠ **9** **Drain** the fish. **Flake** it into a bowl, removing any skin and bones.

⚠ **10** Heat half of the olive oil in a saucepan over low heat. Add the chopped onion, garlic, and eggplant. Add the chili powder (if using). **Fry** for 10 minutes, until the eggplant is soft.

11 Add the flaked fish to the onion and eggplant mixture and mix together well.

12 Spoon a layer of each ingredient into an ovenproof dish in this order:
- potato slices
- fish and onion mixture
- shredded cabbage
- shrimp
- chopped pumpkin
- parsley

13 **Drizzle** the rest of the oil over the top of the dish. **Cover** the dish with foil and **bake** for 30 minutes.

14 Remove the foil and bake for 20 more minutes.

Baked Fish with Lime and Orange Juice

You can use all sorts of different fish in this recipe. It often is cooked with fresh red snapper in the Caribbean, but if you can't find any, try using frozen cod or haddock. If you use frozen fish, move it from the freezer to the refrigerator about 12 hours before you start cooking so it can completely **thaw**.

What you need

2 garlic cloves
1/2 onion
2 green onions
2 limes
1 orange
2 fish fillets
1/2 tsp sugar
1/2 tsp dried thyme
1/2 tsp chili powder
   (optional)
salt and pepper

What you do

1 **Preheat** the oven to 400°F (200°C).

2 **Peel** the garlic clove and onion and finely **chop** them.

3 Cut the tops and bottoms off the green onions and finely chop the rest.

4 Cut the limes and orange in half. Squeeze the juice out of them with a lemon squeezer.

5 Put the fish fillets into an ovenproof dish. Pour 1 cup (200 ml) of water around them.

6 Pour the lime and orange juice over the fish.

7 Put the chopped garlic, sugar, thyme, chopped onion, chopped green onions, chili powder (if using), and a pinch of salt and pepper onto the fish.

8 **Cover** the dish with foil and **bake** the fish for 30 minutes. Serve it with plain rice.

RED SNAPPER

Red snapper is one of the most popular fish in the Caribbean. It is the most common species of snapper, but other species come in different colors and patterns, including striped snapper!

Baked Ground Provisions

The term "ground provisions" is used to describe vegetables that are grown all over the Caribbean, such as sweet potatoes and pumpkins. It suggests using foods that the ground provides.

What you need

$1/3$ lb (150 g) pumpkin
$1/3$ lb (150 g) potatoes
$1/3$ lb (150 g) sweet potatoes
1 14-oz. (400 ml) can coconut milk
$1/4$ lb (100 g) cheddar cheese
1 tbsp butter or margarine
2 tbsp **cornstarch**

What you do

1 **Preheat** the oven to 350°F (180°C).

2 **Peel** the pumpkin, remove the seeds, and cut it into quarters. Thinly **slice** the pumpkin quarters.

3 Peel the potatoes and sweet potatoes and thinly slice them.

4 Put the coconut milk into a saucepan and bring it to a **boil**. Add the sliced potatoes, sweet potatoes, and pumpkin.

5 **Simmer** the vegetables in the coconut milk for 10 minutes.

6 **Drain** the coconut milk from the vegetables into a bowl. Put it aside.

7 Grate the cheese.

8 Melt the butter or margarine in a saucepan over low heat.

22

9 Remove the saucepan from the heat and gradually add the cornstarch, stirring all the time, to make a thick paste.

10 With the pan still off the heat, slowly stir the coconut milk into the paste.

11 Put the sauce back onto the heat and heat gradually, stirring all the time, until it becomes thick and starts to bubble. Stir in the grated cheese and cook for another minute until all the cheese has melted.

12 Arrange the slices of potato, sweet potato, and pumpkin in an ovenproof dish. Pour the cheese sauce over the top.

13 **Bake** in the oven, uncovered, for 25 minutes.

Banana Curry

As with banana soup and chicken and banana skewers, this dish is usually made with plantains in the Caribbean. If you can't find them, use unripe bananas that are still slightly green. Serve this curry with rice.

What you need

1 tbsp butter or margarine
2 tbsp cornstarch
1 14-oz. (400 ml) can coconut milk
$1/4$ tsp nutmeg
1 tsp curry powder
salt and pepper
2 plantains or unripe bananas

What you do

1 **Preheat** the oven to 450°F (230°C).

2 Melt the butter or margarine in a saucepan over low heat. Remove the saucepan from the heat and gradually add the cornstarch, stirring all the time, to make a thick paste.

3 While the pan is still off the heat, gradually stir the coconut milk into the paste. Do this very slowly so you don't get lumps in the sauce.

4 Put the sauce back on the heat and heat gradually, stirring all the time, until it becomes thick and starts to bubble.

5 Add the nutmeg, curry powder, and a pinch of salt and pepper to the sauce and stir.

6 **Peel** the bananas and thickly **slice** them. Arrange them in the bottom of an ovenproof dish.

7 Pour the sauce over the bananas.

8 **Bake** your curry in the oven, uncovered, for 30 minutes.

PLANTAIN CHIPS

Plantains can be **fried**, **boiled**, or baked. Plantain chips—a little like potato chips—are made by cutting plantains into thin slices, then **deep-frying** them and sprinkling them with

25

Bean and Egg Salad

Caribbean cooks use many types of beans. Beans are filling and **nutritious.** This salad contains three different types—red kidney beans, white kidney beans, and green beans. You could eat this salad as a main course, perhaps with some crusty bread.

What you need

1 red onion
2 tbsp olive oil
1 tbsp balsamic vinegar or red vinegar
1 tbsp mayonnaise
$3/4$ cup (200 g) canned kidney beans, drained
$3/4$ cup (200 g) canned white kidney beans, drained
$2/3$ lb (300 g) green beans
2 or 3 large lettuce leaves
2 eggs

What you do

1 **Peel** the onion and finely **chop** it.

2 In a bowl, mix together the oil, vinegar, and mayonnaise.

3 Add the chopped onion and the **drained** red and white kidney beans to the mixture.

4 Cut the ends off the green beans. If the beans are long, cut them in half. Bring a saucepan of water to a **boil** and add the green beans to the pan. Boil them for 5 minutes, then drain the water from the beans and allow them to **cool.**

5 Carefully place the eggs into a saucepan. Add enough water to cover them.

6 Bring the water to a boil, reduce the heat, and **simmer** the eggs for 15 minutes.

7 Use a spoon to lift the eggs out of the water. Hold them under cold running water to cool them, then peel off the shells.

8 Put the lettuce leaves on a plate. Put the bean mixture in the middle of the lettuce leaves.

9 Arrange the green beans in a circle around the bean mixture. **Slice** the eggs and arrange them in a circle around the green beans.

Red, Yellow, and Green Salad

This colorful and refreshing salad is ideal for a hot day. It could be served as a side dish, or you could eat it with crusty bread as a snack or light lunch.

What you need

1 green pepper
1 yellow pepper
1 red pepper
2 large tomatoes
1/2 a head of lettuce, such as iceberg or romaine
1 lime
3 tbsp olive oil
1 tbsp white wine vinegar
2 tsp paprika
2 tsp sugar
salt and pepper

What you do

1 Cut the tops off the peppers and scoop out the seeds. **Slice** the peppers into thin rings.

2 Thinly slice the tomatoes.

3 Shred the lettuce.

4 Arrange the salad in a bowl in layers. Put a layer of green peppers at the bottom, followed by a layer of tomatoes, a layer of yellow peppers, and a layer of red peppers.

5 Top the salad with the shredded lettuce.

28

6 Cut the lime in half. Using a lemon squeezer, squeeze the juice out of one half of it.

7 Put the lime juice, olive oil, vinegar, paprika, sugar, and a pinch of salt and pepper into a small bowl and mix them together to make a dressing for the salad.

8 **Drizzle** the dressing evenly over the salad. Try not to mix it in, or you will spoil the layers you have built.

SERVING THE SALAD

If you can, make this salad in a glass bowl so you can see the different layers through the side of the bowl. When you serve it, use a knife to cut it into colorful wedges.

Coconut Custard

Coconuts are used in many Caribbean dishes. The name coconut comes from a Portuguese word meaning "monkey's face." Perhaps the fifteenth century Portuguese explorers who sailed to the Caribbean thought the three dents on a coconut shell looked like a monkey's face. You need to make this custard a few hours before you want to eat it, so it has time to **chill**.

What you need

1/2 cup (100 ml) cream
2 eggs
1/4 cup (25 g)
    powdered sugar
1/2 cup (100 ml)
    canned coconut milk
1/2 tsp vanilla extract

What you do

1 **Preheat** the oven to 325°F (165°C).

2 Put the cream, eggs, and sugar into a food processor or blender. **Blend** the ingredients on the highest setting until they make a smooth paste.

3 Add the coconut milk and vanilla extract to the mixture and blend together for a few seconds.

(!) 4 Pour the mixture into an ovenproof bowl. Put the bowl into a roasting pan and carefully pour hot water into the pan so that the water comes halfway up the sides of the bowl. **Cover** the whole roasting pan with foil.

30

5 Carefully put the roasting pan into the oven and cook the custard for 1 hour.

6 Take it out of the oven and leave it to **cool** for 2 hours. When it is cold, put it into the refrigerator to **chill**.

COCONUT JUICE

Coconut juice is the **transparent** liquid that forms in the middle of a coconut. It is sold by street vendors all over the Caribbean. The vendor cuts off the top of the coconut with a knife or axe, then sticks a straw into the hole before handing the coconut over to the thirsty customer!

Sweet Potato and Pumpkin Pudding

Sweet potatoes and pumpkins are used in both **savory** and sweet Caribbean dishes. This dessert combines sweet potato and pumpkin with spices and dried fruit.

What you need

1/2 lb (200 g) sweet potatoes
1/2 lb (200 g) pumpkin
1 tsp dried ginger
1/2 tsp nutmeg
1/2 tsp cinnamon
1/2 tsp vanilla extract
1/2 cup raisins
1 tbsp butter or margarine
1/2 cup (100 ml) canned coconut milk
1/3 cup (50 g) brown sugar

What you do

1 **Preheat** the oven to 400°F (200°C).

2 **Peel** the sweet potatoes and pumpkin. **Grate** both of them into a bowl.

3 Add the ginger, nutmeg, cinnamon, vanilla extract, and raisins to the bowl of grated sweet potatoes and pumpkin.

4 Melt the butter or margarine in a saucepan.

5 In a bowl, mix together the coconut milk, brown sugar, and melted butter or margarine. Pour this mixture into the sweet potato and pumpkin mixture and mix everything together.

6 Spray an 8-in (20-cm) round baking pan with cooking spray.

7 Spoon the pudding mixture into the baking pan. **Bake** it in the oven for 1½ hours.

8 Take the pudding out of the oven and let it stand for 10 minutes before serving.

Banana Bread

Banana bread is cooked all over the Caribbean. You could eat it as a dessert with cream or as a snack. It is best to use very ripe bananas.

What you need

3 ripe bananas
1 stick butter or margarine
1 1/4 cups (250 g) brown sugar
1 egg
2 3/4 cups (350 g) self-rising flour
1/2 tsp cinnamon
1/2 tsp nutmeg
1/2 cup (100 ml) milk
1 tsp vanilla extract

What you do

1 **Preheat** the oven to 350°F (180°C).

2 **Peel** the bananas and, using a fork, **mash** them in a bowl.

3 Using a wooden spoon, **beat** the butter and brown sugar together in a bowl. Add the egg and beat the mixture for 1 minute.

4 Add the bananas to the butter, sugar, and egg mixture and mix everything together.

5 Using a metal spoon, **fold** the flour, cinnamon, and nutmeg into the mixture.

6 Add the milk and vanilla extract to the mixture. Stir the mixture well.

7 Spray a 9-in. x 5-in. (22.5 cm x 12.5 cm) loaf pan with cooking spray.

8 Spoon the banana bread mixture into the loaf pan. **Bake** it in the oven for 1 hour.

9 Using an oven mitt, tip the bread out onto a cooling rack. Allow it to **cool** before you slice it.

IS IT COOKED?

You can check whether the banana bread is cooked by sticking a toothpick or knife straight down into the middle of the bread. If the toothpick or knife comes out clean, the bread is ready. If it comes out with some mixture stuck to it, put the bread back in the oven for a few more minutes.

Pancakes with Mangoes

You need a really ripe mango for this dish. Check if it is ripe by squeezing it gently. If you feel it "give," it is ripe.

What you need

1 ripe mango
1 tbsp powdered
  sugar
1 egg
3/4 cup (175 ml) milk
3/4 cup (80 g) white
  flour
1/2 tsp nutmeg
2 tbsp vegetable oil

What you do

1 **Peel** the skin from the mango. Cut the flesh from either side of the flat pit.

2 Put the mango flesh into a food processor or blender with the powdered sugar. **Blend** the mango on the highest setting until it becomes a **pulp.**

3 Spoon the mango pulp into a bowl, then clean the blender.

4 Put the egg and milk into the blender and turn it to its highest setting for about 30 seconds.

5 Turn the blender to low. Gradually pour in the flour and nutmeg. Blend the batter until it is smooth.

6 Put the batter into the refrigerator and allow it to stand for 30 minutes.

7 Heat 1/2 tbsp oil in a medium-sized nonstick frying pan over medium heat. Put 3 tbsp of the pancake batter into the pan and swirl it around so that the batter spreads out.

8 Cook the pancake for about 1 minute. Turn it over and cook the other side for another minute.

9 Slide the pancake out of the pan onto a plate and repeat steps 7 and 8 until you have made four pancakes.

10 Divide the mango pulp between the four pancakes, spreading it over half of the pancake.

11 Fold the other half of the pancake over the top of the filling and fold the pancake again.

37

Mango Ice Cream

It can get very hot in the Caribbean, so ice cream is popular. To make this recipe, you need really ripe mangoes. See page 36 for how to check the ripeness of a mango.

What you need

2 ripe mangoes
1 1/3 cup (300 ml) milk
4 egg yolks
1 cup (100 g) powdered sugar
1 1/3 cup (300 ml) heavy cream

What you do

1 **Peel** the mangoes. Cut the flesh from the pit and put the flesh into a food processor or blender. **Blend** the mango on the highest setting until it becomes a **pulp.**

2 Put the milk into a saucepan. Heat it until it is steaming but not **boiling.**

3 To separate the egg yolks from the whites, carefully crack one of the eggs over a small bowl. Keeping the yolk in one half of the shell, let the white drip into the bowl. Pass the yolk from one half of the shell to the other until all the white has dripped out. Put the yolk in a separate bowl. Repeat with the other eggs. **Beat** the egg yolks and sugar together in a bowl until they are well mixed.

4 Gradually pour the hot milk into the egg and sugar mixture, stirring all the time.

5 Pour the mixture back into the saucepan. Cook it over low heat until it thickens, about 10 minutes.

38

6 Pour the mixture into a bowl, then stir in the cream and the mango pulp with a whisk.

7 Put the mixture into the freezer. After 1 hour, take the bowl out of the freezer and **mash** the mixture with a fork to break up any lumps.

8 Repeat step 7 until the ice cream is set. This should take about 4 or 5 hours, depending on how cold your freezer is.

Ginger Ale

Ginger ale is a popular drink all over the Caribbean. It often is sold by street vendors. The vendors have a huge block of ice from which they chip some ice into a cup. They then pour the ginger ale over the top to make a wonderfully cool and refreshing drink.

Although ginger ale is quick and easy to make, you have to let it stand for a couple of days, so that the taste of the ginger spreads through the whole drink.

What you need

large piece fresh
  ginger (1 oz)
1 3/4 cup (175 g)
  powdered sugar

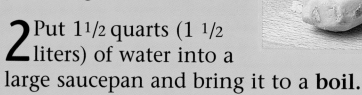

What you do

1 **Peel** the ginger and finely **grate** it. Keep your fingers clear!

2 Put 1 1/2 quarts (1 1/2 liters) of water into a large saucepan and bring it to a **boil**.

3 Add the grated ginger and powdered sugar to the boiling water. Stir everything together, then turn off the heat.

4 Cover the pan and let it stand in a cool place for 2 days.

40

5 Pour the ginger ale through a strainer into a small pitcher, then pour it into a plastic or glass bottle.

6 Keep the bottle in the refrigerator.

GINGER MEDICINE

Ginger is used by many people as a medicine. In the Caribbean, a hot drink made from ginger is used to relieve stomach pains and the flu.

41

Coconut Milkshake

Coconuts are used in many ways in Caribbean life. The flesh of the coconut is an ingredient in a lot of different dishes. There is a liquid in the center of the coconut that people drink. The coconut shell is made into utensils such as spoons and cups, and the leaves of the coconut tree are used to make roofs for houses.

What you need

1 cup (200 ml) vanilla ice cream

1 cup (200 ml) canned coconut milk

1/2 cup (100 ml) milk

1/2 tsp nutmeg

What you do

1 Put all the ingredients into a food processor or blender.

2 **Blend** the milkshake on the highest setting until it is smooth.

3 Pour the milkshake into two glasses. Enjoy!

OTHER MILKSHAKES

You can make milkshakes in all kinds of different flavors. Try replacing the coconut milk with mashed bananas or crushed pineapple.

ADDING ICE

To make your milkshakes even more refreshing on a hot day, put ice cubes in the bottom of the glasses before pouring in the milkshake.

More Books

Cookbooks

Illsley, Linda. *The Caribbean*. Austin, Tex.: Raintree Steck-Vaughn, 1999.

Kaufman, Cheryl Davidson. *Cooking the Caribbean Way*. Minneapolis, Minn.: Lerner Publications, 1989.

McKenley, Yvonne. *A Taste of the Caribbean*. Austin, Tex.: Raintree Steck-Vaughn, 1995.

Books About the Caribbean

Mayer, T.W. *The Caribbean and Its People*. Austin, Tex.: Raintree Steck-Vaughn, 1995.

Shalant, Phyllis. *Look What We've Brought You from the Caribbean*. Parsippany, N.J.:Silver Burdett Press, 1998.

Comparing Weights and Measures

3 teaspoons = 1 tablespoon	1 tablespoon = 1/2 fluid ounce	1 teaspoon = 5 milliliters
4 tablespoons = 1/4 cup	1 cup = 8 fluid ounces	1 tablespoon = 15 milliliters
5 1/3 tablespoons = 1/3 cup	1 cup = 1/2 pint	1 cup = 240 milliliters
8 tablespoons = 1/2 cup	2 cups = 1 pint	1 quart = 1 liter
10 2/3 tablespoons = 2/3 cup	4 cups = 1 quart	1 ounce = 28 grams
12 tablespoons = 3/4 cup	2 pints = 1 quart	1 pound = 454 grams
16 tablespoons = 1 cup	4 quarts = 1 gallon	

Healthy Eating

This diagram shows which foods you should eat to stay healthy. You should eat 6–11 servings a day of foods from the bottom of the pyramid. Eat 2–4 servings of fruits and 3–5 servings of vegetables a day. You should also eat 2–3 servings from the milk group and 2–3 servings from the meat group. Eat only a few of the foods from the top of the pyramid.

Caribbean cooking uses many ingredients from the bottom of the pyramid. For example, people often eat rice as part of their main meal. The rest of the meal might consist of chicken, fish, or beans, along with vegetables such as pumpkin, plantains, or peppers. Fruits are used in sauces and desserts. Fats, oils, and sweets are not main ingredients in Caribbean cooking.

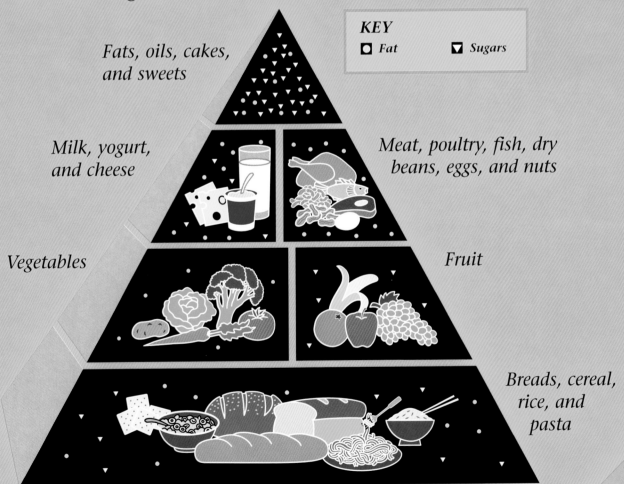

Fats, oils, cakes, and sweets

KEY
◻ Fat   ▽ Sugars

Milk, yogurt, and cheese

Meat, poultry, fish, dry beans, eggs, and nuts

Vegetables

Fruit

Breads, cereal, rice, and pasta

Glossary

bake to cook something in the oven

beat to mix something together strongly, for example egg yolks and whites

blend to mix ingredients together in a blender or food processor

boil to cook a liquid on the stove until it bubbles and steams strongly

broil to cook something over or under an open flame

bouillon cube small cube of powdered meat or vegetable powder used to make a base for soups or sauces

chill to put a dish in the refrigerator for several hours before serving

chop to cut something into pieces using a knife

cool to allow hot food to become cold, especially before putting it in the refrigerator

cornstarch powder made from corn that is used to thicken sauces and puddings

cover to put a lid on a pan or foil over a dish

deep-fried cooked at a high temperature in deep, hot oil

dissolve to stir something, such as sugar, until it disappears into a liquid

drain to remove liquid from a can or pan of food

dressing cold sauce for a salad

fry to cook something by placing it in hot oil or fat

grate to shred something by rubbing it back and forth over a utensil that has a rough surface

marinate to soak something, such as meat or fish, in a mixture before cooking so that it absorbs the taste of the mixture

mash to crush something, for example a potato, until it is soft and pulpy

nutritious food that is good for our bodies and our health

peel to remove the skin of a fruit or vegetable

preheat to turn on the oven in advance, so it is hot when you are ready to use it

pulp mixture that has been mashed or blended until smooth

savory dish that is not sweet

simmer to cook a liquid on the stove just under a boil

slice to cut something into flat pieces

staple main ingredient, one found in many dishes

stock broth made by slowly cooking meat or vegetables in water or by dissolving a cube of meat flavoring in water

thaw to bring something that has been frozen to room temperature

transparent see-through

Index